Coolidge

JP

# NUGGET & FANG

We Rule!

ME

YOU

Tammi Sauer          Michael Slack

Houghton Mifflin Harcourt
Boston   New York

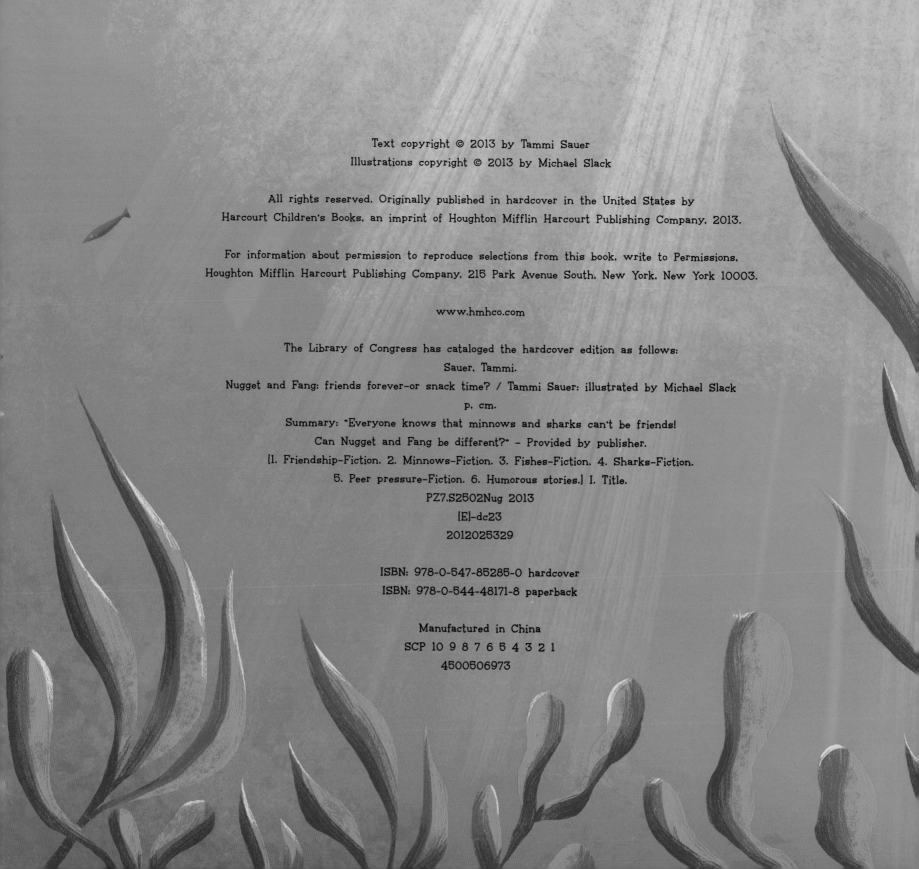

For information about permission to reproduce selections from this book, write to Permissions,
Houghton Mifflin Harcourt Publishing Company, 215 Park Avenue South, New York, New York 10003.

www.hmhco.com

The Library of Congress has cataloged the hardcover edition as follows:
Sauer, Tammi.
Nugget and Fang: friends forever—or snack time? / Tammi Sauer: illustrated by Michael Slack
p. cm.
Summary: "Everyone knows that minnows and sharks can't be friends!
Can Nugget and Fang be different?" – Provided by publisher.
[1. Friendship–Fiction. 2. Minnows–Fiction. 3. Fishes–Fiction. 4. Sharks–Fiction.
5. Peer pressure–Fiction. 6. Humorous stories.] I. Title.
PZ7.S2502Nug 2013
[E]–dc23
2012025329

ISBN: 978-0-547-85285-0 hardcover
ISBN: 978-0-544-48171-8 paperback

Manufactured in China
SCP 10 9 8 7 6 5 4 3 2 1
4500506973

For the fang-tastic Mason and Bryant—T.S.

For Nola Belle—M.S.

In the deep, deep ocean
lived two best friends.
Nugget and Fang.
They did everything together.

They swam over.
GLUG

They swam under.
GLUG-GLUG

BOO!

They swam all around.
GLUG-GLUG-GLUG

Life was close to perfect . . .

until it was time for Nugget to go to school.

On Monday, Nugget was busy with . . .

READING

"Today's story is about three little minnows and a big, bad shark . . ."

"A big, *bad* shark?
Ha!" said Nugget. "Impossible."

THE THREE LITTLE MINNOWS

Nugget was busy with . . .

# MATH

$$1+1=2$$
$$2+2=4$$

But what if there were ten minnows and a shark came along and ate four of them?

How many minnows are left?

"Is this a trick question? A shark would never do that!" said Nugget.

And Nugget was busy with . . .

SCIENCE

"Sharks are scary.
Here's the proof!"

MARINE FOOD CHAIN

SHARK

"The stuff on that poster isn't true," said Nugget.
"My best *friend* is a shark!"

HAVE YOU LOST YOUR GILLS?

SHARKS AND MINNOWS CAN'T BE FRIENDS!

HELLO—SHARKS EAT MINNOWS!

Nugget was shocked. (And apparently delicious.)

That afternoon, Nugget explained it all to Fang.
"Sharks are toothy. Sharks are scary.
Sharks and minnows can't be friends."

NUGGET
**Food Chain Test**

1. Sharks eat: A+

a. Minnows
b. Rusty license plates
c. Surfers
d. All of the above

"Sounds fishy to me," said Fang.
"It's true. See?" said Nugget.
He held up his test.
Then he swam far, far away.

Fang's heart sank.
There was nothing he could do about being toothy.

But he needed his best buddy back.
He had to prove he wasn't scary.

On Tuesday, Mini Minnows had a surprise visitor.
A very BIG surprise visitor.

The visitor gave Nugget his friendliest smile.

SHARK!
SWIM FOR
YOUR LIVES!

"Oh, my algae!" said Nugget. "It's Fang."

On Wednesday, Fang tried a different approach.

Dear Nugget,
I'd love to
have you over
for dinner.
Sincerely,
Fang

HE WANTS

TO EAT

YOU

"Holy mackerel!" said Nugget.

FOR

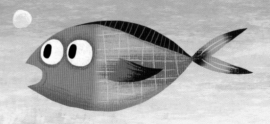

DINNER!

On Thursday, Fang tried everything he could think of.

A tattoo.

A special delivery.

A song and dance.

THE WILD SEA HORSES

But nothing worked.

On Friday, Fang was out of ideas.

All alone, he swam over.
*BLUB*

He swam under.
*BLUB-BLUB*

He swam all around.
BLUB-BLUB-THWUMP

Life was not even close to perfect.

Fang was so busy boo-hooing,
he didn't notice a net drop

down,

down,

down . . .

right on the mini minnows!

OH, NO!

The net pulled up, **up, up.**

SOMEBODY, HELP!

Fang squinted. "Nugget?"
He had to do something. But what?

Fang fanned his gills.
He wrung his fins. Then . . .

PING!

Fang had a plan.

Fang's big sharp teeth chomped.
Fang's big sharp teeth chewed.

Fang saved the mini minnows!

All the minnows stared.

"I know, I know," said Fang.
"I'm toothy. Too scary. Too . . . shark."

Nugget swam toward Fang.
"There were ten minnows," he said, "and a very special shark came along. How many friends are there altogether?"

There was only one answer.

In the deep, deep ocean lived eleven friends.

They swam over.
*GLUG*

They swam under.
*GLUG-GLUG*

They swam all around.
GLUG-GLUG-GLUG

And everyone was all smiles.
Especially you-know-who.